For Kayla and Zinnia,
forever my first readers
–S.B.

For Esther
–M.M.

Visit us on the Web! rhcbooks.com

Educators and librarians, for a variety of teaching tools, visit us at RHTeachersLibrarians.com

Library of Congress Cataloging-in-Publication Data
Names: Briseño, Stephen, author. | Mora, Magdalena, illustrator. | Title: The notebook keeper : a story of kindness from the border / by Stephen Briseño ; illustrated by Magdalena Mora. | Description: First edition. | New York : Random House Studio, [2022] | Includes bibliographical references. | Audience: Ages 4–8. | Summary: After traveling to Tijuana, Mexico, Noemi and her mother are denied entry at the border and must find the refugee in charge of the notebook, an unofficial ledger of those waiting to cross into the United States. Includes author's note. Identifiers: LCCN 2021040297 (print) | LCCN 2021040298 (ebook) | ISBN 978-0-593-30705-2 (hardcover) ISBN 978-0-593-30706-9 (library binding) | ISBN 978-0-593-30707-6 (ebook) | Subjects: CYAC: Emigration and immigration—Fiction. | Border stations—Fiction. | Kindness—Fiction. | LCGFT: Picture books. Classification: LCC PZ7.1.B757425 No 2022 (print) | LCC PZ7.1.B757425 (ebook) | DDC [E]—dc23

The text of this book is set in 14-point Delima MT Pro.
The illustrations were rendered using colored pencil, pastel, gouache, and Photoshop collage.
Interior design by Rachael Cole

MANUFACTURED IN CHINA
10 9 8 7 6 5 4 3 2 1
First Edition

the Notebook Keeper

A STORY OF KINDNESS FROM THE BORDER

Stephen Briseño & Magdalena Mora

RANDOM HOUSE STUDIO
NEW YORK

Mamá tells me we have a long way to walk.

Before, sunshine drenched the yard. Our neighbors' laughter danced in the streets.

Now, Papá is gone. The streets are unsafe. We are leaving, too.

Our home is no longer a home. "Have faith, mi vida," Mamá says.

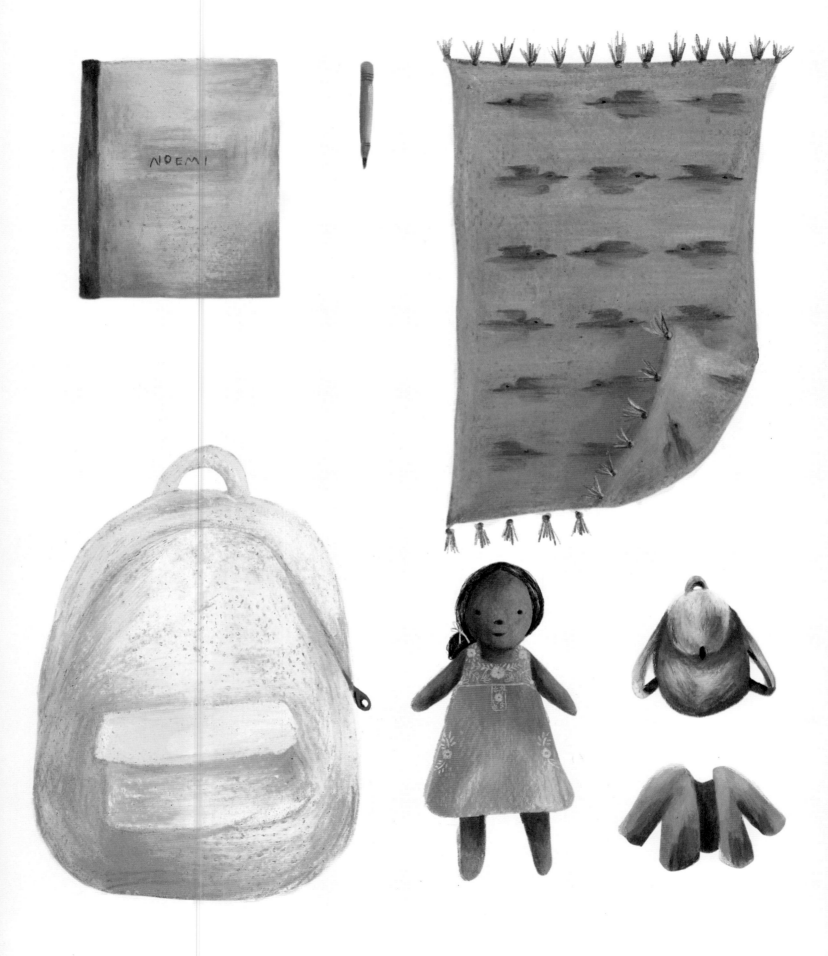

I pack only what I can carry.

My blanket.

My notebook.

And my muñeca.

At first our walk is lonely.

But our group gets bigger.

And more colorful.

When we arrive, we are not greeted with kindness.

"You cannot go through today. Go find the notebook keeper. Get your names into the notebook. She will tell you when you can cross."

I ask Mamá what the man means.

But Mamá is silent.

A crowd waits.

Mamás. Papás. Abuelas and abuelos.

Children like me.

It's hard to see any kindness here.

Until I meet the notebook keeper.

"Buenos días, amigas. My name is Belinda. Please tell me your name and your country."

Belinda opens her notebook. Nombres and números fill the pages.

"And who are you, chica? Where are you from?"

"My name is Noemí. I am from Mexico."

"I am glad you are here, Noemí. Don't worry. You will cross soon. Your number is 653."

"653. 653." I repeat the number over and over.

653

1	Agustín Flores	Guatemala
2	Enrique Mejía	El Salvador
	Jerome Reyes	El Salvador
3	Fernanda García	Puebla
4	Manuela Morales	Guerrero
5	Araceli Rojas	Michoacán
	Noemí Jiménez	Michoacán
6	Jesús Salazar	Venezuela
7	Fermín Ortega	Puebla
8	Daniel Cadet	Haití

654

1	Simon Jean-Baptiste	Haití
2	Wesley Guillame	Haití

We settle into a new life.

Our home is different. Not like it used to be.

Our dinner is different. Not like we used to have.

Mamá is different, too. Her eyes are dark with worry.

"Will we be called tomorrow, Mamá?"

"No se, Noemí. I don't know."

Once the sun rises, Belinda calls out:

"574, Cano. 574, Saldaña. 574, Treviño."

Most are allowed through.

Some return.

Even though my heart hurts, Belinda encourages us.

"Please, everyone, tengan fe. Your number will be called soon. I am just like you. I, too, am waiting for my number to be called. Have patience."

I wonder how Belinda can keep her smile. I feel mine fading every day.

"Why are you so happy doing this job, Belinda?" I ask.

"This is not my job, Noemí. I am a volunteer."

"You are?"

"A man named Tomás from Guatemala chose me to be the next notebook keeper once his number was called. And when I hear my own number, I will choose someone to take *my* place."

"How will you know who to pick?"

"I will choose someone with generosity in their heart and kindness in their soul," Belinda says.

"But how will you find this person? How will you know?"

She is silent.

Days turn into weeks.

I worry that our
day will never come.

I wish there were more people like Belinda here.

I make a choice.

One day, Belinda's number is called.
I am sad—but happy, too.

"I believe you two are the ones to take care of this for us."

It's hard saying goodbye to Belinda, our notebook keeper.
I wonder what will happen to her.
I wonder when our number will be heard.

But Mamá and I will encourage, remind, and comfort.
Like Belinda did.

For those who are here.

For those who wait.

For those who still have a long way to walk.

AUTHOR'S NOTE

For the thousands of refugees who have gathered at the San Ysidro Border Checkpoint in Tijuana, Mexico, for entry into the United States, Noemí's story is familiar.

At this checkpoint, a refugee was chosen to manage the notebook, an unofficial ledger containing the names of those seeking asylum. When new arrivals came, the notebook keeper wrote down their name and country and gave them a number, usually assigned to many different families. And they waited.

Each morning, U.S. Customs agents notified the notebook keeper of how many refugees would be allowed to plead their case for asylum. The notebook keeper then called those next in line by last name and number.

At the end of the day, the notebook was given to a representative from Grupos Beta, the humanitarian arm of the National Institute of Migration of Mexico, for safekeeping.

Families waited in line for weeks or even months for their number to be called, fleeing from persecution, poverty, and violence. Even then, many were denied entry to the United States, forced to find hope elsewhere.

Once the notebook keeper's number was called, a new keeper was chosen from among those in line.

No one is exactly certain how the San Ysidro notebook system began, and as of the writing of this story, it is no longer in operation. It ended with the outbreak of the Covid-19 pandemic in 2020, when the border closed.

Notebook keeper Jose Cortes of El Salvador
in Tijuana, Mexico, June 20, 2018

SELECTED SOURCES

Brayman, L. and Langellier, R. (2018). "The Notebook: Asylum Seekers Improvise a
New Border Bureaucracy." *The Nation.* thenation.com/article/notebook-border-tijuana

Carcamo, C. (2018). "For many waiting in Tijuana, a mysterious notebook is the key to
seeking asylum." *Los Angeles Times.* latimes.com/local/california
/la-me-asylum-seekers-notebook-holds-key-to-entry-20180705-story.html

Sieff, K. and Kinosian, S. (2018). "For migrants in Tijuana, seeking asylum in U.S. starts
with a worn notebook." *The Washington Post.* washingtonpost.com/world
/the_americas/for-asylum-seekers-in-tijuana-fellow-migrants-are-organizing
-force/2018/11/27/41028e0a-f1bb-11e8-99c2-cfca6fcf610c_story.html

This American Life (2019). "Let Me Count the Ways." thisamericanlife.org/656/let-me-count
-the-ways